The Dragons
of Kangaroo Island

ISBN 1 8766 77 58 9

First published by:
 Tangara Publishing
 8314 Greenwood Avenue
 PMB 14
 Seattle
 Washington 98103
 USA

Design and Production by:
 Publishing Solutions
 38A Murphy Street
 Richmond, VIC 3121
 Australia
 email: solve@publishing-solutions.com.au

Author contact details:
If you have enjoyed this book and would like to write to Jacqui, please send an email to the following address:
 wolfeellady@earthlink.net

Photo Credits

Clockwise from top of *Life Cycle*

Leafy Sea Dragon	© Tony White	New Hatchling	© Tony White
Weedy Sea Dragon with eggs	© William Tan	Juvenile Leafy Sea Dragon	© Tony White
Detail of egg mass	© William Tan	Leafy Sea Dragon	© William Tan
Small Leafy hatching from egg	© Tony White	Giant Cuttlefish	© Jacqueline Stanley

Acknowledgements

Thanks to Jim Thiselton for his interest and advice, and William Tan for his generous spirit and talent.
Thanks to my family for their love and enthusiasm, especially my husband, Rod.

Editing

Suzanne Bastedo and Kevin Jeans

References

SA. Lourie, ACJ. Vincent and H. Hall (1999) *Seahorses: an identification guide to the world's species and their conservation*. Project Seahorse, London
RH. Kuiter (2000) *Seahorses. Pipefishes and their relatives: a comprehensive guide to Syngnathiformes*. TMC Publishing, Australia
B. Hutchins and R. Swainston (1986) *Sea Fishes of Southern Australia*. Western Australian Museum, Australia

The Dragons
of Kangaroo Island
More Adventures of an Undersea Creature

Written and Illustrated by Jacqueline Vickery Stanley
Foreword by Jim Thistleton

AUSTRALIA

■ Adelaide

GREAT SOUTHERN OCEAN

Lightmeter Cove

KANGAROO ISLAND

FOREWORD.

To Everyone with an interest in life in our precious oceans,
Welcome to Jacqui's children's book on Sea Dragons.

As I write this foreword, I am sitting on our dive boat, now at anchor in "Lightmeter Bay".

The emotion and sentiments aroused by the reading of Jacqui's latest book are quite real, especially to me, as Kangaroo Island is my home. I spend a lot of time on my farm here on Kangaroo Island, but my real love is the Great Southern Ocean that surrounds this island and the marine creatures that inhabit its waters especially the Weedy and the Leafy Sea Dragons.

The Sea Dragons are two unique creatures, much as discussed in the pages to follow. They have individual personalities, just like you and me. The human characteristics of the two Sea Dragons in *The Dragons of Kangaroo Island* underscore that individuality. Children of all ages will be able to experience how life can be for the creatures beneath the waves and that sometimes it is not all that different to life on the surface!

Since 1993, we have enjoyed assisting divers to visit our Weedy and Leafy Sea Dragons in their natural habitat. Kangaroo Island is one of the very few places around the vast coast of Australia, where it is possible to see both species of Sea Dragons. By observing the Sea Dragons we hope to learn far more about these incredible creatures and how best to protect them.

Through the story of *The Dragons of Kangaroo Island* readers will discover that marine creatures come in a variety of shapes, sizes and colors. Each creature has its own special place and purpose in our magnificent ocean world.

Jacqui, I wish you well in your endeavors to bring knowledge and understanding to readers of all ages.

Best wishes,

Jim Thiselton.

Jim Thiselton and his wife, Josie, own *Kangaroo Island Diving Safaris* and offer a wonderful experience, both above and below the surface, of a unique part of Australia.

It was a windy, dark day on Kangaroo Island. Huge waves crashed against the big, grey cliffs that rose up above the Great Southern Ocean. White foam flew back across the sea.

Near the small bay at the top end of Kangaroo Island, furry kangaroos huddled together to keep warm. Little joeys peeked out of their mother's pouches. High up in the eucalyptus trees, koalas were sound asleep, curled up in tight little balls. Glossy black cockatoos sat near them with their feathers fluffed up to keep out the cold wind.

Under the Great Southern Ocean it was a gloomy day. The water surged back and forth and back and forth. Big beds of kelp moved back and forth with the surges. Schools of black-and-white Old Wife fish that lived near the kelp, were feeling a bit seasick. Finally they all decided to move down to a small cave where they began to feel better.

E ven deeper in the water, where the kelp met the white sand, Lucille, the Weedy Sea Dragon was hunting for tiny mysid shrimp. Mysid shrimp were her favorite food.

Lucille was a beautiful Weedy Sea Dragon. Her gold and brown body had spots and purple stripes along the sides. Around her long neck she had a small fin to help her move gently through the water. She had another fin along her back. Lucille had a long, elegant snout and a small, pretty mouth that she used to suck up thousands of tiny mysid shrimp. She had to suck very hard because Lucille had no teeth. On her head and down her back and tail Lucille had small fins that looked a lot like wings. They helped her hide in the kelp so she could ambush the mysid shrimp that lived there.

Lucille's body was thin, except in the middle. Lucille did not like her middle at all. Almost every day she complained to her father about the way her body looked.

"I wish I could change my body," she would say. "I want to be long and thin all over." Lucille would look down at her middle and sigh.

"Your body is made in this special way to protect you." Lucille's father would explain.

"Your skeleton is arranged in hard rings around the outside of your body. It protects your body and your fins help you to hide in the kelp." He would say.

"If you did not look like this you would not be a Weedy Sea Dragon. You must be proud of how you look." Her father tried so hard to change her mind.

But Lucille didn't listen to her father.

4

She kept trying different ways to change her shape. Sometimes, she would just try as hard as she could to pull her middle in but with a hard skeleton on the outside, it didn't work. Her skeleton stayed the same shape. Sometimes, she faced into the current hoping it would push in her middle. That didn't work either. She also tried not eating so many mysid shrimp. All that happened was she got so hungry she ate twice as many shrimp as before!

At least a hundred times each day, Lucille wished that she looked like her cousin, Leslie. Lucille thought he was beautiful. He didn't have a big middle.

"If only I could hide my middle," she said to herself. "If only I had more fins like Leslie I could hide it."

Leslie was a Leafy Sea Dragon. Leslie did look a lot like Lucille but Leslie was draped in glorious green and gold fins. Everywhere on his body he had special, wonderful fins. He even had fins at the end of his snout! The fins looked exactly like the leaves of the kelp.

Like Lucille, Leslie spent much of his time moving slowly through the kelp hunting the tiny mysid shrimp. They were his favorite food too. Lucille liked to find Leslie and just look at him. She would drift near him and cover her middle with kelp and pretend that she had lots of fins, just like Leslie. Then she felt beautiful and special like Leslie.

Back up on Kangaroo Island, a horrible rumbling noise was disturbing the animals and birds that lived near the bay. The kangaroos hopped away looking for a place to hide. The joeys tucked themselves deeper into their mother's pouches. The koalas stopped munching on eucalyptus leaves and blinked in amazement. The glossy black cockatoos flew away screeching in alarm.

They had all heard this noise before but it was so loud that it always frightened the birds and animals that lived near the bay. It was a huge, old grey truck. The truck belonged to Mr. Thistleberry who loved to take divers under the water to see the most special creature in the waters around Kangaroo Island. The special creature was The Leafy Sea Dragon. Kangaroo Island was one of the only places in the whole world where Leafy Sea Dragons lived. Divers came from everywhere to dive with Mr. Thistleberry. He always knew just where to find the Leafy Sea Dragons.

Down in the bay, the door of the truck screeched and Mr. Thistelberry's voice boomed across the water.

"O.K. divers, let's get all this gear into the boat!"

Four people jumped down from the truck. They began to carry tanks and bags and facemasks and fins and underwater cameras down to the little white boat that waited in the bay. It took many trips back to the truck to get everything loaded in the boat. By the time they had finished, the wind that had been blowing all morning had stopped. The sea became calmer. It was going to be a great day for diving. Mr. Thistleberry started the engine and headed the little boat out of the bay and around the coast of Kangaroo Island.

Soon, the boat arrived at Lightmeter Cove and Mr. Thistleberry dropped the anchor. The divers began dressing into their underwater gear. They already wore wet suits. These suits would help keep them warm under the water. Over their wetsuits they pulled on their buoyancy compensators and tanks. They all had hoses attached to the tanks which lead to regulators that the divers placed in their mouths so they could breathe. To see properly under the water, the divers wore masks on their faces. To help them swim, they wore fins on their feet. Some divers wore gloves and hoods to help keep them warmer. Finally, the divers were all ready. One by one they dropped into the sea. PLOP! PLOP! PLOP! PLOP!

From the boat, Mr. Thistelberry handed the divers their cameras and their underwater flashes. Then, he rolled over the side of the boat and into the water. PLOP!

He looked at the four divers bobbing in the sea and made a signal pointing his thumb down. That was a sign for all the divers to go under the water. With Mr. Thistleberry leading the way, the divers all swam down and down. When they reached the bottom they all gave him a sign with their fingers to show that they were O.K. Mr. Thistleberry swam off with the divers following him.

Lucille had heard the boat engine stop and she heard PLOP! PLOP! PLOP! PLOP! and PLOP!

"Oh no, here we go again," she said to herself.

It was hard for Lucille to feel beautiful and special when the divers came to take photographs. First Mr. Thistleberry would arrive. He thought Lucille was beautiful and he wanted to show the other divers. Mr. Thistleberry would make a loud noise with an underwater whistle. The noise was very, very loud. The other divers would come swimming over to see what Mr. Thistleberry had found as fast as they could.

Every time, Lucille saw the same looks appear on the divers' faces. They wanted to see a Leafy Sea Dragon, like Leslie, not a Weedy Sea Dragon, like her. They always took many pictures of Leslie. Sometimes the divers watched Lucille for a few moments and maybe even took a few pictures of her. But then they always swam away searching for Leafy Sea Dragons. Lucille knew they were disappointed. She was sure the divers didn't want to take pictures of her because she had a big middle.

Claude, the Giant Cuttlefish saw Lucille's sad face. Whenever the divers came, Claude would drift over to talk with Lucille. He often tried to cheer her up by demonstrating his new camouflage ideas. Claude was huge. He was much bigger than Lucille. Around his face waved long arms dotted with suckers. Lucille thought Claude was terribly clever. She loved watching him change color from red to green to yellow in the blink of an eye. Not only that, but Claude could change his shape to look like the kelp or the coral!

Claude had a lot of things to think about. Not only did he have to manage his color changes and body changes but he had to operate his jet propulsion moves. Claude used this move to get away quickly from his enemies. If Claude's jet propulsion moves did not work, he still had another trick to use. Claude could squirt a large cloud of ink to confuse his attacker. Claude was always busy, but he was a good friend to Lucille and tried hard to think of ways to make her feel better.

"At least we have good eyesight," he said to her one day. "Leslie can't see much for weeks after all the cameras flash in his face. He bumped into me three times last week!"

Just as Claude the Giant Cuttlefish was saying this, he and Lucille heard the underwater whistle. Then they saw flashes of light near the kelp bed. The divers had found Leslie.

The flashes went on for a long time. As usual, the divers stayed near Leslie as long as they had film in their cameras and as long as the air in their tanks lasted.

"Maybe my eyesight is good," Lucille grumbled to Claude that day, "but what good is that if no one notices me? I want to be special."

"You are special, Lucille," Claude said. He sighed. But, like her father, Claude had told her this many times before. "You belong to the only Weedy Sea Dragon family in the world."

Nothing Claude said made her feel better. Lucille was so envious. She wanted the divers to take many pictures of her too. If only she was thin and had lots of green and gold fins like Leslie.

Then, one day, Lucille had an idea. If she stayed with Leslie all the time and draped enough kelp around herself, the divers would think that she was a Leafy Sea Dragon too!

In the next days and weeks, Lucille spent all her time with Leslie. She missed talking with Claude and watching him change color. Lucille missed the rest of her Weedy Sea Dragon family too. They had been places. Some had been all the way around Kangaroo Island. Some had even traveled half way around Australia. They always had lots of interesting stories to tell.

Leslie was beautiful, but boring. He had always stayed in the same place. He had never left Lightmeter Cove at Kangaroo Island. He didn't have any interesting stories to tell. In fact, he hardly talked at all! But Lucille had set her mind on looking and acting like a Leafy Sea Dragon. She copied everything that Leslie did. Soon, Lucille began to feel that she really was a Leafy Sea Dragon. Lucille was ready for the divers. She could hardly wait.

Finally, one day Lucille heard the underwater whistle. Then she saw clouds of bubbles rising up not far from where they were drifting in the kelp. She could hear the bubbles too!

"Leslie!" squealed Lucille. "Look! The divers are coming! The divers are coming!"

She was so excited.

As usual, Leslie just kept drifting in the kelp. Lucille moved closer to him. Then she pulled some golden kelp around her. Suddenly, Mr. Thistleberry appeared. He became very excited. When he saw Leslie and Lucille he waved at the other divers and sounded the loud underwater whistle. When all the other divers had arrived, Mr. Thistleberry held up two fingers. He pointed first to Leslie and then to Lucille.

Lucille turned to Leslie and whispered, "He thinks I am a Leafy Sea Dragon too!" She was so happy.

The divers aimed their cameras at Leslie. FLASH! The flash went off. Leslie sighed and closed his eyes.

Then it was Lucille's turn. FLASH! FLASH! Before she knew it, Lucille couldn't see anything. The divers were all around them and the flashes kept popping.

Like Leslie, Lucille shut her eyes tight.

Finally, it felt quiet and dark again. Lucille opened one eye. She couldn't see much at all except circles of bright light, but she could tell that the divers had gone.

Suddenly, Lucille felt a bump.

"Watch out! Where do you think you are going?" a voice shouted.

Squinting, Lucille turned around and saw the grumpy face of a small Rough Bullseye Fish.

"Sorry!" said Lucille. She tried to drift away but got tangled up in the kelp. She still couldn't see very well. It felt very scary but at least she was popular!

After a long time, Lucille's eyesight cleared. She quickly pulled the kelp around her body and swam to the edge of the white sand. She was never going to let anyone see that she was a Weedy Sea Dragon again. It felt so good to be special.

From then on, every time Lucille heard the underwater whistle, she rushed into the kelp bed and pulled the kelp around her. She smiled at the cameras and swam a little, just like Leslie. Lucille was so happy.

One night Lucille woke up. Had she heard the underwater whistle? Was she dreaming? No! There it was again! Lucille looked to see whether Leslie was awake too, but he was snoring quietly in the kelp.

Then as the divers came closer, she saw that Mr. Thistleberry was not with them. None of these divers had cameras.

"I wonder what they want at this time of the night?" Lucille whispered to Leslie.

Leslie kept snoring. Lucille moved closer to him, and pulled the kelp around her. Even if these divers did not want to take pictures, she wanted to look her best. She rubbed her eyes and peered at the divers.

As the divers came closer still, Lucille noticed that one held a big net. The diver swam over to Leslie, who was still fast asleep. Lucille moved even closer to Leslie and swished the kelp around so the divers would see her. She didn't want to be left out.

All of a sudden, Lucille and Leslie were scooped up in the net. Lucille could feel herself moving up and up, away from the kelp bed. They were going up fast. Too fast. Lucille felt dizzy.

"Why are we going up so quickly?" she whispered to Leslie. But he kept snoring.

Lucille looked down. She couldn't even see the kelp bed any more. She realized that these divers did not want to take pictures of her and Leslie. They wanted to TAKE THEM AWAY FROM THEIR HOME!

Lucille rushed around in the net. The diver squeezed the top of the net with his hand and Lucille couldn't get out. She bumped against Leslie.

"Wake up!" Lucille yelled. Leslie opened one eye.

"I don't feel very well." He moaned. " Please help me."

His eyes closed. Lucille noticed that Leslie's glorious gold and green fins were no longer floating, but were hanging down like dead brown kelp. Leslie's fins did not look beautiful at all. And Leslie wasn't swimming with his head up as he always did. Instead, his head was hanging down and his belly floated up.

Lucille was worried. Again and again, she swam up to the big fist of the diver at the top of the net and then back down to Leslie. She did not know what else to do.

Suddenly, Lucille realized they had stopped moving up.

"We are saved!" she cried to Leslie

Then, the net with Leslie and Lucille in it was taken out of the water. Leslie was lying at the bottom of the net. He looked very very sick. Lucille felt sick too. She was still dizzy and she could hardly move. Suddenly, they were plopped into water. It felt good to be back into the water again but everywhere Lucille swam she bumped into something hard. She soon realized that they were in a very, very small ocean.

Lucille began to cry.

" I don't want to be a Leafy Sea Dragon. Leslie! Leslie! LESLIE! WAKE UP!" Lucille screamed. Leslie didn't move.

Lucille knew she had to do something. She tried to think. Then she heard a noise.

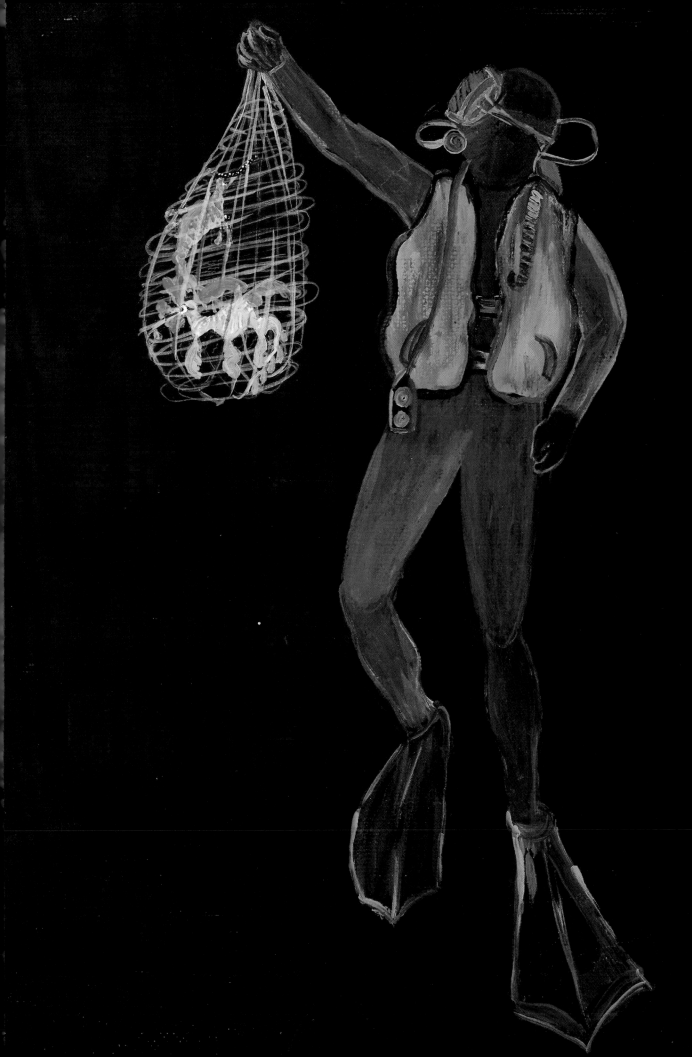

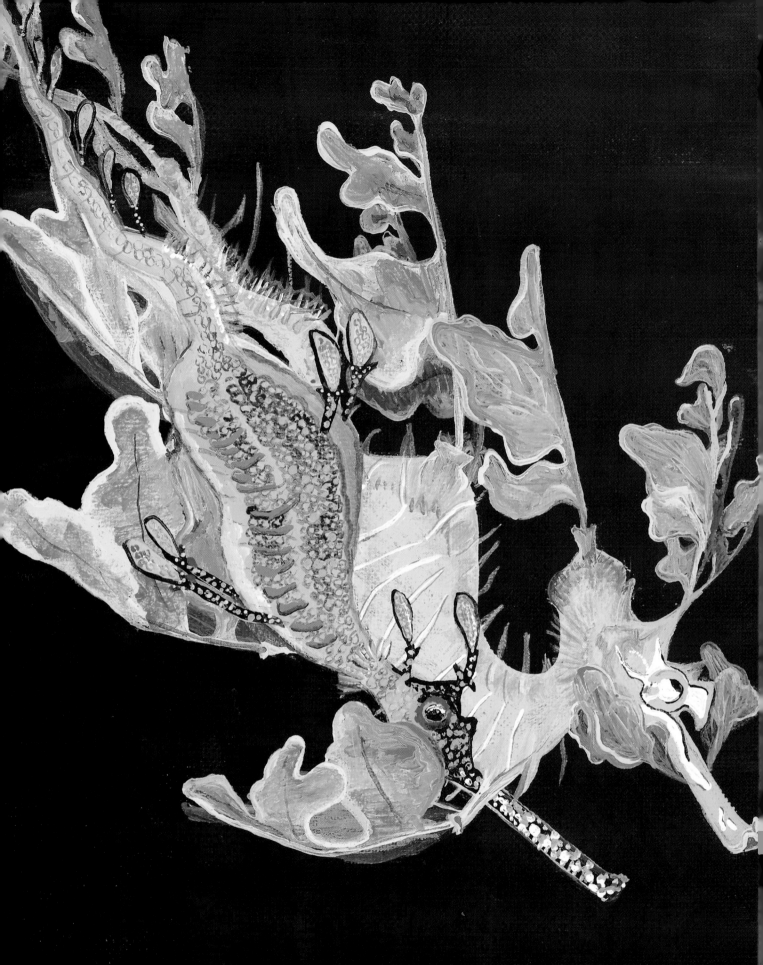

"Let's see what we have in this pail."

Lucille looked up and saw five faces looking down at them. At first they smiled. Then the faces showed the same disappointed look that Lucille had seen many times before.

"We don't want that Weedy, just the Leafy." One face said.

"Yeh," the other face agreed. "We won't get much money for a Weedy. Throw the Weedy back."

The water sloshed over the side of the pail. Lucille felt herself start to fall out. She looked down and saw the big ocean. She thought fast.

Lucille kept letting herself fall out, but at the last minute she pushed her long, elegant snout under one of Leslie's kelpy fins. With a swoosh, Leslie slid up from the bottom of the pail. Lucille nudged him again and they both fell back into the Great Southern Ocean.

PLOP! PLOP!

As fast as she could, Lucille pushed Leslie down to the kelp. As they went deeper, his fins began to lose their droopy look, but he still couldn't move much. Lucille swam as fast as she could. She nudged Leslie down, down towards the bottom. She listened carefully in case the divers were following them.

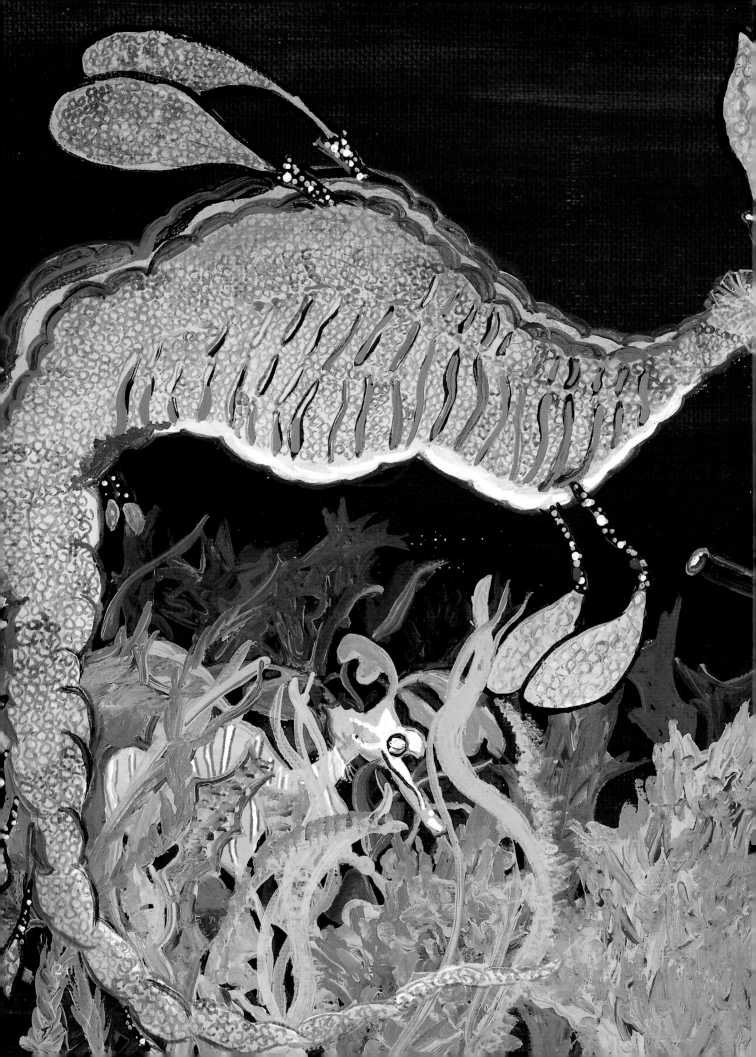

When Lucille and Leslie reached the bottom, Lucille looked around frantically for some kelp. Luckily, they were right near a small patch and Lucille pushed Leslie into the golden weeds.

Then she swam to the edge of the white sand. She stopped and tried to catch her breath. Just as she was staring to feel safe, she heard a noise.

Oh No! She could hear bubbles again! The divers were coming back! There was no kelp to hide her!

Then Lucille smiled to herself. "I don't have to worry", she thought. They don't want me because I am not a Leafy Sea Dragon. That's why they tipped me back into the ocean.

The divers came closer. Lucille swam away from the kelp. She tried to show as much of her middle as she could. She wanted to let the divers see that she was a Weedy Sea Dragon, not a Leafy Sea Dragon.

When the divers reached Lucille, they shone their underwater flashlights on her. They saw her gold and brown body with spots and purple stripes along the sides. They saw the small frilly fin around her long neck. They saw her big middle. They saw that she was a Weedy Sea Dragon. They shook their heads and they swam past her and past Leslie who was hiding in the kelp behind Lucille.

"Thank you, Lucille." Leslie whispered, when the divers had gone. He had woken up and was feeling much better. "You saved my life. Those divers captured my mother last year. It is very dangerous being a Leafy Sea Dragon." Leslie gave Lucille a big leafy hug.

"You're welcome Leslie!" Lucille was surprised. She had never heard Leslie say so much before.

L ucille waved goodbye to Leslie and swam away from the kelp. She couldn't wait to tell her friend Claude the Giant Cuttlefish all about her adventures. As she swam, she looked down at her gold and brown body. She admired her purple stripes and her spots and especially her big, important middle. Lucille thought that she did look a lot like her father. After all, she did belong to the Weedy Sea Dragon family. Lucille wiggled her fins, and her mouth watered at the thought of all the mysid shrimp she would soon be sucking up with her long, elegant snout. Lucille felt beautiful, just the way she was.

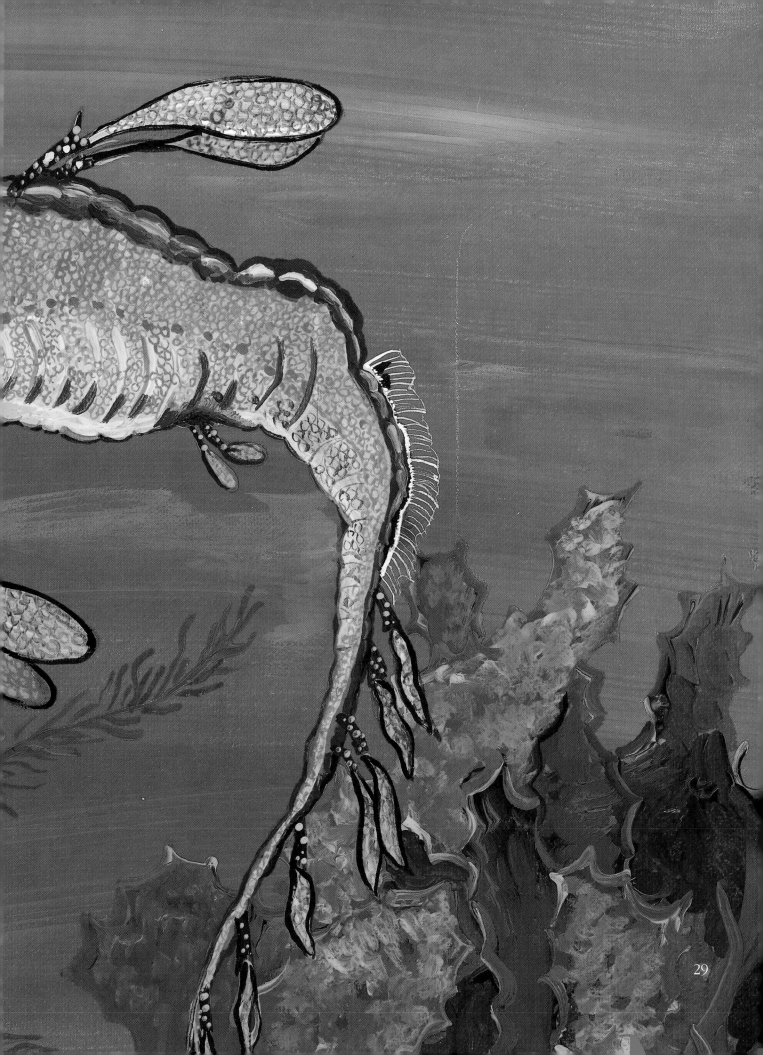

The female deposits eggs by pushing them on to the tail of the male.

Sea Dragons grow to full size in 2 years.

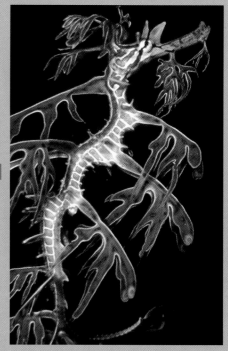

Juvenile Leafy Sea Dragon at approximately 6 weeks.

Males carry the eggs for 2 months.
They can carry about 250–300 eggs.

Eggs are embedded in the skin of the tail.

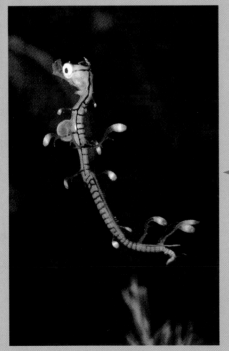

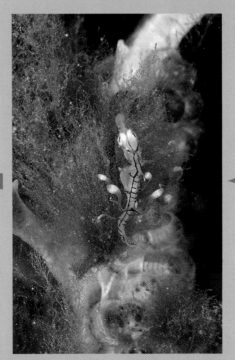

They come out tail first and are
ready to swim in a few hours.

After 2 months the young
hatch.

THE DRAGONS OF KANGAROO ISLAND QUESTION AND ANSWER SHEET

SEA DRAGONS

1 To which Family do Sea Dragons belong?

The Leafy Sea Dragons (*Phycodurus eques*) and their cousins, the Weedy Sea Dragons (*Phyllopteryx taeniolatus*), are the only Sea Dragons in the world that inhabit temperate waters and along with sea horses and pipefishes, are members of the family Sygnathidae.

These are fish with a hard external skeleton, arranged in a series of rings around the animal's body. Sea Dragons also have long tubular snouts and no teeth. One way to tell Sea Horses and Sea Dragons apart is that Sea Horses can coil up their tails, but Sea Dragons cannot. Sea Dragons swim horizontally.

2 Where and how do Sea Dragons live?

Sea Dragons live from five to seven years and live in the waters of the Southern Australian coastline. Weedy Sea Dragons can grow as long as 20 inches (51 cm) and Leafy Sea Dragons can grow to 18 inches (46 cm).

Weedy Sea Dragons range from the southeastern coast, down around Tasmania, and across the Great Australian Bight to the southwestern coast of Australia. Leafy Sea Dragons stay in a much smaller area. They are found only from Kangaroo Island to the southern coast of Western Australia. The Leafy and the Weedy Sea Dragons are the only Sea Dragons in the world that inhabit temperate waters, between 58°–65°F (14°–20° C).

They live from between 15–70 feet (5–20 metres) and even deeper below the water's surface, where the kelp grows. The kelp provides camouflage and this is where their favorite food, the mysid shrimp live. Each shrimp is about the size of a grain of sand. The Sea Dragons strike at these very small shrimp by expanding a joint on the lower part of their snout causing a suction force that sucks the shrimp in.

3 How do Sea Dragons reproduce?

The most interesting thing about Sea Dragons is that it is the male who carries the young and gives birth to them. The female lays between 200 and 300 eggs at one time under the tail of the male. She then swims with the male and pushes the eggs into the skin of his tail. The eggs fit into cups and the male will carry them for between 46 to 48 days. The male will hatch a few baby Sea Dragons at a time over a wide area. Once born, the babies leave at once and move to shallow water where they feed on small zooplankton.

4 Why do Sea Dragons have so many fins?

Weedy Sea Dragons have fins that are part of their bony skeletons. These fins are a bit like fingers or toes are for humans. Because they look like kelp, these fins help with camouflage. But the Weedy Sea Dragon moves around far more than the Leafy Sea Dragon, and so camouflage is not as important.

Because the Leafy Sea Dragon does not move very much at all, camouflage is very important. The Leafy's fins look like kelp. These fins help hide the Leafy Sea Dragon from enemies, and also from the Leafy's favourite food — the tiny mysid shrimp.

5 Who are the Sea Dragon's enemies?

Humans are the main enemy of Sea Dragons. Sea Dragons are often caught in nets of fishing boats while many also die as a result of pollution and excessive fertilizer run-off.

Sea Dragons are also taken from Australian waters illegally for home aquariums all over the world. Many often die as these aquariums are not equipped to manage them properly and they are extremely sensitive to changes. Aquarium-raised Sea Dragons are usually exported to public aquariums.

Storms are another enemy of the Sea Dragon. They can be found washed up on the beach, caught up in seaweed after a bad storm.

6 Are Sea Dragons Protected?

Yes. The Leafy Sea Dragon was declared a "totally protected species" in 1991. The leafy Sea Dragon is the official conservation symbol of southern Australian waters

Members of the public are encouraged to report any findings of Sea Dragons to an organization called Dragon Search.

GIANT AUSTRALIAN CUTTLEFISH

1   Which Family do the Giant Australian Cuttlefish belong ?

Giant Australian Cuttlefish belong to the group of creatures called *cephalopods* as do Octopus and Squid. The name cephalopod comes from the Greek words for head — *kephale*, and foot, — *podos*. The name describes the Giant Cuttlefish as being part head and part foot.

There are approximately one hundred species of cuttlefish known in the world and the Giant Australian Cuttlefish is the largest.

2   Where and how do the Giant Australian Cuttlefish live?

Giant Australian Cuttlefish live between approximately 18 months to 2 years. They can reach lengths of over three feet (1 metre). They live only in the southern waters of the coast of Australia and are found along the coast from the Spencer Gulf in South Australia to the waters off Sydney in New South Wales.

The Giant Australian Cuttlefish has a very big appetite. It feeds on small fish, crabs and prawns and also on other cephalopods.

The Giant Australian Cuttlefish is a clever hunter. It distracts its prey by making its arms come to a point or sometimes even raising two arms above its head. Then, it shoots out its secret weapon, which are two special feeding tentacles that are kept in pouches underneath its eyes. When the Giant Australian Cuttlefish has caught its prey, the special feeding tentacles are put away and the cuttlefish holds the prey with its arms and uses its powerful beak to break the prey into bite-sized pieces.

The Giant Australian Cuttlefish has jet propulsion. It pulls water through its body up into its head and then forces that water through a special funnel. The funnel has a swivel, which helps the cuttlefish to steer.

3   How do Giant Australian Cuttlefish reproduce?

During the mating season, the male Giant Australian Cuttlefish display a brilliant colour to attract a female. The male cuttlefish have to fight and the toughest competitor will mate with the female. The male and female cuttlefish mate when the male passes a sealed sperm package to a pouch beneath the female's mouth. Then the female enters a den and takes each of her eggs, which are the size of ping-pong balls, and passes it over the sperm package. The eggs are then hung up on cave roofs in clusters. They are pure white.

The Giant Australian Cuttlefish lay about 200 eggs. The eggs hatch after 4 months and the tiny cuttlefish look exactly like their parents. Shortly after laying the eggs the female Giant Australian Cuttlefish dies.

4   How do Giant Australian Cuttlefish change their colour and skin texture?

The messages to change colour or skin texture enter the brain of the Giant Australian Cuttlefish and then that message is sent to cells called chromatophores.

Each chromatophore is a small dot of colour when it is relaxed. When the chromatophore expands so does the dot of colour and so the Giant Australian Cuttlefish changes colour when all the cells receive the message to change.

5   Who are the enemies of the Giant Australian Cuttlefish?

Many fish and dolphins like to prey on cuttlefish. The cuttlefish are also caught by commercial fishermen to use as bait or sold to restaurants for human consumption.

It is not known what effect this fishing is having on the Giant Australian Cuttlefish population. There is a great need to study the life-cycle of the Giant Australian Cuttlefish.

FISHES

OLD WIFE FISH

Why are they called Old Fish Wife and where are they found?

They are called Old Wife Fish because they have a habit of grinding their teeth together when they are caught. Fishermen believe that the sound resembles the grumblings of an "old wife'. They are common in coastal reef and weedy areas of Southern Australia and especially around Kangaroo Island.

Old Wife Fish have dorsal spines along the top of their bodies which are venomous and are capable of inflicting a painful wound.

ROUGH BULLSEYE FISH

Why are they called Rough Bulleye Fish and where are they found?

They are called Rough Bullseye Fish because they have scales that are very small and very rough to touch. They have a bright orange bar at the rear of their heads, which looks like a bullseye. They are found in the waters off the coast of Southern Australia and especially around Kangaroo Island.

KANGAROO ISLAND

1 Where is Kangaroo Island?

Kangaroo Island is the third largest island off the coast of Australia. It is 75 miles (155 km) long and up to 26 miles (55 km) wide and covers an area of 2796 miles (4500^2 km). Kangaroo Island is situated off the tip of Cape Jervis, near Adelaide in South Australia.

2 What animals can be seen on Kangaroo Island?

Kangaroo Island was part of the mainland of Australia until 9500 years ago. Since then many plants, animals and birds have survived in isolation with some even evolving differently from the mainland species. More than half the area of the island has never been cleared of vegetation. Vast areas of bushland remain undisturbed and are free from destructive rabbits and foxes and have abundant wildlife.

Native wildlife can be seen in its natural habitat on Kangaroo Island as the island has over 20 National Parks.

Some of the animals that are seen on Kangaroo Island include; The Kangaroo Island Tree Kangaroo; the Short-Beaked Echidna; the Southern Brown Bandicoot; the Tammar Wallaby; the Rosenberg's Sand Goanna; the Platypus and Koalas.

Underwater sea creatures include the Leafy Sea Dragon; the Weedy Sea Dragon; the Giant Australian Cuttlefish; the Australian Fur Seal and the Australian Sea Lion.

Kangaroo Island also has many species of birds. Some birds that can be seen are: Little Penguins; Purple-crowned Lorikeets; Superb Fairy-Wrens; Crimson Rosellas and the only population of the Glossy Black Cockatoo.

3 What Plant and Insect life can be seen on Kangaroo Island?

There are wildflowers to be found in every season on Kangaroo Island. Australia's floral emblem, the Golden Wattle, flowers in the spring. There are more than 850 species of plants on the island. All wildflowers are protected.

Kangaroo Island is home to the Ligurian Bee which was brought over to Kangaroo Island in 1881 and since that time no other bees have been introduced to the island. Due to the isolation of Kangaroo Island all the bees are descendents of those original hives, are pure Ligurian and are unique in the world.